Smile, Lily!

For Lillian Grace, who always makes me smile – C. F.

For Auden and Sara Jane – Y. H.

First published in Great Britain in 2004 by Pocket Books,
an imprint of Simon & Schuster UK Ltd.
Africa House, 64-78 Kingsway, London WC2B 6AH.

Originally published in 2004 by Atheneum Books for Young Readers,
an imprint of Simon & Schuster Children's Publishing Division, New York.

Text copyright © 2004 by Candace Fleming. Illustrations copyright © 2004 by Yumi Heo.

The rights of Candace Fleming and Yumi Heo to be identified as the author and illustrator of
this work have been asserted by them in accordance with the Copyright, Designs and Patents
Act, 1988.

Book design by Polly Kanevsky
The text for this book was set in
Graham.
The illustrations are rendered in oils,
pencil, and collage.

A CIP catalogue record for this book
is available from the British Library
upon request.

ISBN 0743478746

Manufactured in China.

10 9 8 7 6 5 4 3 2 1

Smile, Lily!

CANDACE FLEMING
illustrated by YUMI HEO

Pocket Books
London

Lily wakes up crying.

Waa! Waa! Waa!

Lily wakes up crying.
Oh, who knows what to do?

"I do,"
says Lily's mummy.

She sings a doh-ray-mi.
She hums of far-off places.
She hums in every key.
She presses Lily to her heart,
and rocks her in a chair.
"Husha. Husha," Mummy croons.
"There. There. There."

But Lily keeps on crying.

Waa!
Waa!
Waa!

Lily keeps
on crying.
Oh, who knows
what to do?

"I do," says Lily's daddy.

He takes her in his arms.
He swings her gently left and right.
He swings her all around.
He tickles Lily's tummy,
and he holds her way up high.
"Superbaby!"
Daddy whoops.
"Fly! Fly! Fly!"

But Lily keeps on crying.

Waa! Waa! Waa!

Lily keeps on crying.
Oh, who knows what to do?

"I do", says Lily's grandma.

She lays Lily on her back.
She unsnaps Lily's poppers.
With a snap, snap, snap.
She powders Lily's bottom,
and she nibbles Lily's feet.
"You smell delicious,"
Grandma sighs.
"Sweet. Sweet. Sweet."

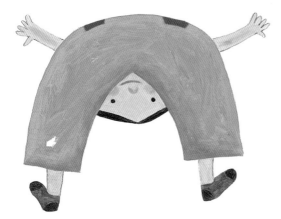

But Lily keeps
on crying.

Waa!
Waa!
Waa!

Lily keeps on crying.
Oh, who knows
what to do?

"I do", says Lily's grandpa.

He sits Lily in her chair.
He spoons a bite of oatmeal.
He spoons a bite of pear.
He chugs the spoon to Lily's mouth,
makes silly noises too.
"Here's the choo-choo!"
Grandpa says.
"Woo! Woo! Woo!"

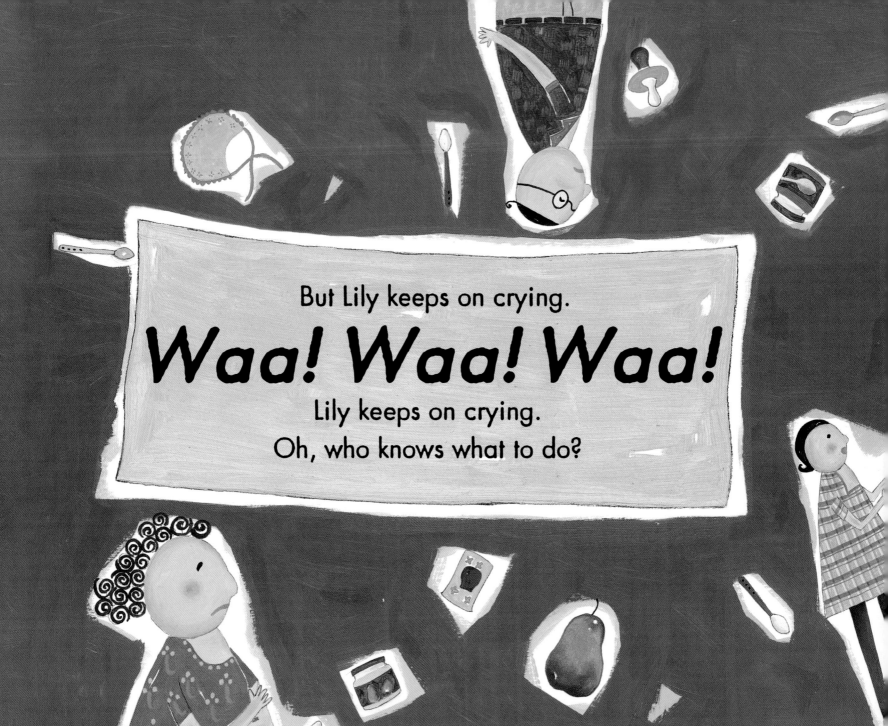

But Lily keeps on crying.

Waa! Waa! Waa!

Lily keeps on crying.
Oh, who knows what to do?

"I do,"
says Lily's uncle.

He rides Lily on his knee.
He shakes her favourite rattle.
He shakes her plastic keys.
He hides his face behind his hands,
and pops out. . .

peekaboo!

"I see you, Lily,"
Uncle plays.
"You! You! You!"

But Lily keeps on crying.

Waa!
Waa!
Waa!

Lily keeps
on crying.
No one knows
what to do!

"Call the doctor!" Mummy panics.
Daddy grabs the phone.
Grandma says a little prayer.
Grandpa starts to groan.
Uncle paces up and down. . .

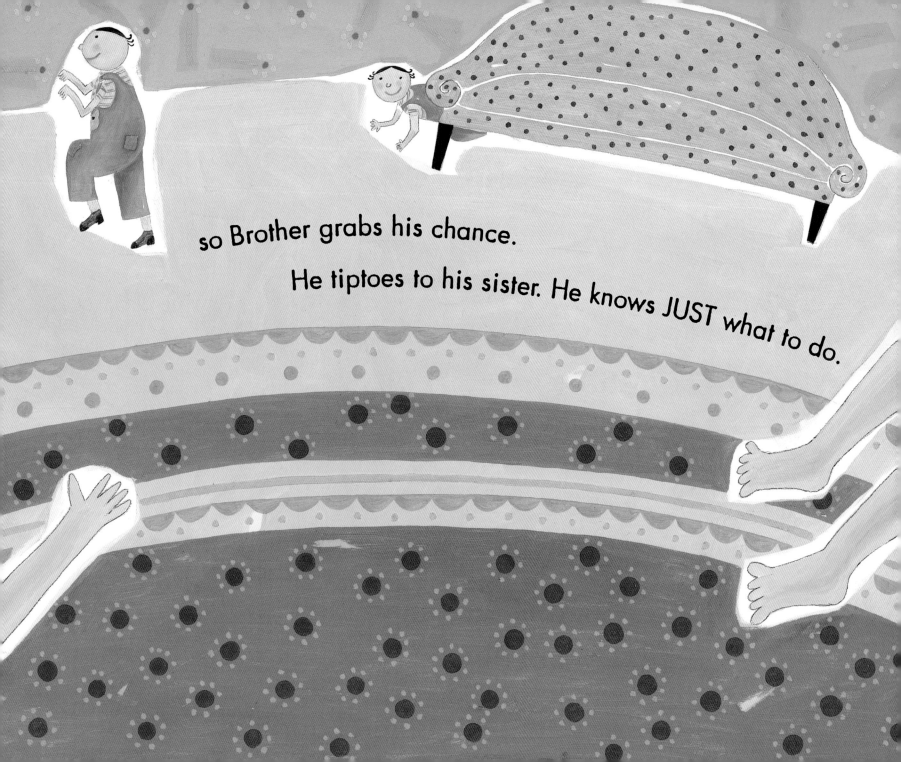

so Brother grabs his chance.

He tiptoes to his sister. He knows JUST what to do.

And with everybody smiling,
Lily smiles too!